Maurice Francis Egan

Songs and Sonnets

And Other Poems

Maurice Francis Egan

Songs and Sonnets
And Other Poems

ISBN/EAN: 9783337181659

Printed in Europe, USA, Canada, Australia, Japan

Cover: Foto ©Andreas Hilbeck / pixelio.de

More available books at **www.hansebooks.com**

✻ SONGS AND SONNETS AND OTHER POEMS BY MAURICE FRANCIS EGAN

A. C. McCLURG AND COMPANY
CHICAGO ✻ ✻ MDCCCXCII

CONTENTS.

SONGS AND HYMNS.

CONTENTS.

NARRATIVE POEMS.

SONNETS.

CONTENTS.

SONGS AND HYMNS

SONGS AND HYMNS.

THE OLD VIOLIN.

HOUGH tuneless, stringless, it lies there in dust,

Like some great thought on a forgotten page;

The soul of music cannot fade or rust—

The voice within it stronger grows with age;

Its strings and bow are only trifling things—

A master-touch!—its sweet soul wakes and sings.

LIKE A LILAC.

LIKE a lilac in the spring
　　Is my love, my lady-love;
Purple-white, the lilacs fling
　　Scented blossoms from above:
So my love, my lady-love,
　　Throws soft glances on my heart;
Ah, my dainty lady-love,
　　Every glance is Cupid's dart.

Like a pansy in the spring
　　Is my love, my lady-love;
For her velvet eyes oft bring
　　Golden fancies from above:
Ah, my heart is pansy-bound
　　By those eyes so tender-true;

Balmy heartsease have I found,

    Dainty lady-love, in you.

Like the changeful month of spring

    Is my love, my lady-love;

Sunshine comes and glad birds sing,

    Then a rain-cloud floats above:

So your moods change with the wind,

    Like the colors of the dove,

All the sweeter, to my mind;

    For the changes, lady-love.

AMONG THE REEDS.

MONG the reeds, beside a singing fountain
    Silenus sat, when life was young and gay,
And piped until the echoes from the mountain
    Awoke the birds as if at break of day.

The fount is dry, and no more old Silenus
    Makes singing sweet re-echo on the shore.
Great Pan is dead; the exiled fauns have seen us
    Walk with bowed heads, where blithe they danced before.

A DUET IN WINTER.

OME, close your eyes and let us dream
together

That June-time's glow is here;

See not the coming of the snow's first feather,

Hear not the wind's voice drear.

Oh, let's float back to where the roses tremble,

And breezes lift your hair;

And these pink asters,—do they not resemble

The climbing roses there?

You will not dream? How, then, can you
remember

The month that bore our love,

Or taste its sweetness in this dark December,

All gloom the mistress of?

The asters faint are but the ghosts of roses
  (Hold, see them not, I meant),
And no fern-frond in all the land uncloses;
  The summer's gold is spent.

How can we keep the past and drink its
    sweetness,
  How walk in love's dear ways,
If in this winter-cold and incompleteness
  We dream not of June days?

Love is, you say, no child of change and
    season,—
  He is our heart's desire;
Dreams will not keep him: take a woman's
    reason,
  And make a warmer fire.

MANY IN ONE.

O the red and the white and the blue,
　　here's a health!
　To the old and the young and the man
　　that's to be,
Not fame will I wish them or plenty of wealth,
　Nor peace without honor, nor quiet that's
　　not free
To the North, to the South, to the East, to
　　the West,
　To the blue and the gray,—they're all one
　　color now,
To the poor men that work and the rich men
　　that rest;
　To the men of the pen and the men of the
　　plow!

Here's a health to them all, from wherever
they come!
May they learn one short lesson by head
and by heart,—
That the figures are weak till they make up a
sum,—
That the whole is a whole and a part is
a part,—
The red and the white and the blue are but
One,
And the flags of all nations were dipped
in the sea
When their children set face to the westering
sun,—
No Teuton, no Celt,—all Americans we.

FROM THE GRAVE.

EEP not for me, O tender heart!

Thou know'st my wish that all thy part

In life should be a happy way

As sunlit as a summer day.

      Weep not for me!

In life thy tears were bitter drops,

In death thy woe's a hand that stops

The current of Eternity,

And smites thy echoed grief to me,

      O tender heart!

No tears, O love! be happy now!

"A little while," and know shalt thou

What 't is to lie and wait in earth

The resurrection and the birth.

      Weep not for me!

FADED LEAVES.

E heard a maiden singing in a wood,
　He saw the wild vines kiss her as she
　　　stood,
With face upturned to note their wavy grace.

There was no note of sadness in her song,
And yet his thoughts were saddened, as along
The woodland path she went, 'mid tender
　　　leaves.

"To-day's a dream, to-morrow's real," he said;
"For life's a dream, the wakened ones are dead;
She sings a lullaby for all her race."

And death is real, for life is but to-day;
To-morrow's death, to-day will pass away,
And hold, for green and sunlit, faded leaves.

THE SHAMROCK.

HEN April rains make flowers bloom
    And Johnny-jump-ups come to light,
And clouds of color and perfume
    Float from the orchards pink and white,
I see my shamrock in the rain,
    An emerald spray with raindrops set,
Like jewels on Spring's coronet,
    So fair, and yet it breathes of pain.

The shamrock on an older shore
    Sprang from a rich and sacred soil
Where saint and hero lived of yore,
    And where their sons in sorrow toil;
And here, transplanted, it to me
    Seems weeping for the soil it left

The diamonds that all others see

    Are tears drawn from its heart bereft.

When April rain makes flowers grow,

    And sparkles on their tiny buds

That in June nights will over-blow

    And fill the world with scented floods,

The lonely shamrock in our land—

    So fine among the clover leaves—

For the old springtimes often grieves—

    I feel its tears upon my hand.

TO-DAY.

O-DAY is bright with golden gleams of
spring,

To-day is fair, and all our sweet hopes sing;

But night comes down, and then our day is
done.

It is not always bright, nor always spring,

And sunny seasons are the ones that bring

Most sudden showers; and the light is gone!

Live in the sunlight, in the fair to-day!

To-morrow keeps to-morrow, and the way

May, in a moment, lose the light of sun!

OF LIFE.

E, fixing eyes of hope upon the sun,

And never steering while the swift

waves run,

Him turning as they list, can reach no goal.

For all our life is made of little things,

Our chain of life is forged of little rings,

And little words and acts uplift the soul.

'T is good to look aloft with ardent eyes,

And work as well; he, doing these, is wise;

But one without the other gains no goal.

O HEART OF EXILE.

FRANÇOIS COPPÉE.

 HEART of exile, dream thou of the day

When the fair future all thy nature

stirred,

And in thy hand her white hand nestling lay,

Like a tired bird!

Ah, then, how quickly all thy soul within

Grew warm and trembled in that tender hour,

How silently thou drank'st the moments in,

Like a faint flower.

Again dark clouds of sorrow fill thy sky,

For she, afar, can give no look or word—

Thy tender thoughts away all drooping fly,

Like a tired bird.

Already o'er thy soul comes winged distrust,

And grief is born anew in love's late bower,

Thou knowest love will fall and fade in dust,

Like a faint flower.

APPLE BLOSSOMS.

THE tender branches sway and swing,

Whispering all that the robins sing

Of hope and love, and lightly fling

Showers of apple blossoms.

A head of black and a head of gold,

Her little hands in his firm hold,

Eyes that speak more than words have told

Under the apple blossoms.

Ever on earth again shall they

Find in springtime so fair a day?

Is it true that love can pass away

With spring and apple blossoms?

DRIFTING.

T harvest, when the sun shone o'er the
wheat,
  Standing in shocks in the quiet, pleasant
  fields,
We, hand in hand, walked through the noonday heat,
  Along the land to where the pond lay
  still,
  'Neath water-lilies floating at their will.

And while we walked and spoke of other days,
  At harvest, too, before my love and I
Had been made one to walk through this
  world's ways
  As man and wife, until the end shall be,
  When life shall live itself eternally

Her sister, speaking to her, softly said:

 "How far," she asked, "my dear one, have
  you solved

Life's problem? Well, I mind me ere were wed
 Your love and you, you often thought it
  o'er,

 Afraid of darkness on the unseen shore."

And, as we skirted the sweet, verdant shores,
 And drifted near the lilies, spoke no word

My thoughtful wife, and the unmovèd oars
 Caught in the branches of the hanging
  trees

 Came from the land the murmuring hum
  of bees.

"Life is no problem," said my wife, at last;
 "'Tis our own blindness makes us think
  it one;

For we can read the future by the past.

 Has God not kept us? We are anchored

 here,

 Floating, yet anchored—lilies in a mere."

"GOLD AND GREEN."

OLD and green and blue and white,
    Daisies, buttercups and sky,
Grass, and clouds, and birds unite
In a chorus of delight,
    For the tender spring is nigh,
    Soon will winds no longer sigh.

March and April pass away,
    And the dainty-fingered rain
Plays sweet symphonies all day,
Welcoming the lovely May;
    Soon will chickweed fill the lane,
    And poppies sprout amid the grain.

BENEATH A BALCONY,

(AFTER A PERSIAN SONG.)

ARCISSUS-FLOWERS, drunk with
     dews of night,
Her eyelids droop to veil a scornful light,
     And on her fair brow curl the black
        love locks,
     Twin serpents on the pale orb of the
        moon.

O breath of roses, rose of red and white,
O voice of bulbul in the wooded height,
     I care not if her languid smile but mocks,
     A smile from her is Allah's greatest boon.

I only dream !—her veil close hides her face,
The jealous curtain of a holy place;

A rose's hundred leaves on heart of gold
Are not so careful of the gem they hold.

If she should smile and wear a veil of lace,
Another man might look,—such looks deface
    And make a treasure common; sweet the
        fold
    That wraps her from me—and the vile
        and bold!

SLEEPING SONG.

EN months had passed since rosy
Herakles

Had opened wondering eyes unto the sun,

When, in the sloping light of summer's eve,

Alcmena, mother of the little twins,

The hero and his brother fair to see,

Bared her soft breasts, as all our mothers did,

In tender love, and gave her boys their food;

And having laved them in the mellow stream,

She laid them down within Amphytrion's
    shield—

A half sphere of bright brass by bold blows
    won

From slaughtered Pterilaus — then, with
    hands,

Like blush-rose petals, on the head of each,

In tones like cithern-echoes, thus she sang:

"Sleep, my boys, in gentle dewy sleep,

Until the dawn in glowing beauty peep

To call the hours from out the night's dark
>   deep
>   Into the light.

Sleep, for the day has sunk in the red west;

Sleep, 'neath the mother-heart that loves you
>   best;

Sleep, sleep, and peaceful, peaceful be your
>   rest
>   Till dark is light.

Anemones and roses drop their leaves

In silent night, but still the ocean heaves;

And so my heart fresh waves of love receives
>   Through all the night.

My other self in two, my heart in two,

Sleep happy, and wake joyous. Oh, for you

I pray the gods to give me all I sue

   Through day and night!"

And as sea-nymphs soft toss a favored boat,

She rocked the buckler, singing as it moved.

CYCLOPS TO GALATEA.

SOFTER than lambs and whiter than
    the curds,
  O Galatea, swan-nymph of the sea!
Vain is my longing, worthless are my words;
    Why do you come in night's sweet
      dreams to me,
And when I wake, swift leave me, as in fear
The lambkin hastens when a wolf is near?

Why did my mother on a dark-bright day
    Bring you for hyacinths a-near my cave?
I was the guide, and through the tangled way
    I thoughtless led you; I am now your
      slave.

Peace left my soul when you knocked at my
heart—
Come, Galatea, never to depart!

Though I am dark and homely to the sight—
A Cyclops I, and stronger there are
few—
Of you I dream through all the quick-paced
night,
And in the morn ten fawns I feed for you,
And four young bears: O rise from grots
below,
Soft love and peace with me for ever know!

Last night I dreamed that I, a monster gilled,
Swam in the sea and saw you singing
there:
I gave you lilies and your grotto filled
With the sweet odors of all flowers rare;

I gave you apples, as I kissed your hand,

And reddest poppies from my richest land.

Oh, brave the restless billows of your world:

　They toss and tremble; see my cypress-

　　grove,

And bending laurels, and the tendrils curled

　Of honeyed grapes, and a fresh treasure-

　　trove

In vine-crowned Ætna, of pure-running rills!

O Galatea, kill the scorn that kills!

Softer than lambs and whiter than the curds,

　O Galatea, listen to my prayer:

Come, come to land, and hear the song of

　　birds;

　Rise, rise, from ocean-depths, as lily-fair

As you are in my dreams! Come, then, O

　　Sleep,

For you alone can bring her from the deep.

And Galatea, in her cool, green waves,

    Plaits her long hair with purple flower-

      bells,

And laughs and sings, while black-browed

    Cyclops raves

    And to the wind his love-lorn story tells:

For well she knows that Cyclops will ere long

Forget, as poets do, his pain in song.

FRANKNESS.

INCONSTANT? And why not, O fair
    Hélène?
You have the bluest eyes I've ever seen,
Blue as the violets in that season when
    The fields and hills are tinged with faint-
        est green;
But you have not fair Marie's tender voice,
Or Constance's smile, in which all hearts
    rejoice.

Inconstant? Why? I love the good in all,
    The good in one, and like the roving bee,
(Are you *bas bleu*, fair lady, will you call
    My "roving bee" a threadbare simile?)
I go from flower to fruit, and I love each,
The faint-tinged rose-bud and the carmine
    peach.

I love you for your eyes, O fair Hélène,

    Your blue, blue eyes, so deep and limpid-
        clear,

In whose deep depths are drownèd many
        men,

    And for their deaths have you not shed a
        tear!

And yet I love dear Rosalind's shy grace,

And—can I help it?—little Celia's face.

I love the good in all, the good in one;

    Too frank am I? Can't help it! 'tis my
        way.

If you'll be Clytie, I will be the sun,

    And you can follow me about all day,

And yet I'll smile on all, and that will be

Love universal, not inconstancy.

Conceited? How you wrong me, fair Hélène;

    I'm not Apollo, and I know that well.

But you're not Clytie; if you were, why then

    I'd follow you. Good gracious! who

        could tell

The girl would get so mad! A temper, true!

I'll never trust in meekest eyes of blue!

AFTER THE SUMMER.

"Yield up, O love, thy crown and hearted throne."—OTHELLO.

HE walks in vain by yonder garden-gate,
    Where hollyhocks and tall carnations
        rise,
Sweet marjoram, and blooms that linger late,
    And all the scented herbs that house-
        wives prize.

A late rose throws soft kisses to the breeze,
    On petals sunrise-hued, like his love's
        cheeks;
He hears a child's voice in the apple-trees;
    He starts! Ah, no; it is not she that
        speaks.

Gone! Lost! Her voice must ever be afar—
　　Those tones that made his fond heart fer-
　　　vent bound;
'T was not a voice as other voices are,
　　For blithesome hope and love were in the
　　　sound.

She was a damsel, dainty, fair, and fine;
　　A princess in the city's latest style;
And " darts " and " hearts " were not much in
　　her line;
　　A little nonsense was: so, many a mile

Stretches　between　the　lonely　heart　that's
　　left,
　　With fading hedges, and the maiden fair,
One heart is wild with pain, of joy bereft,
　　The　other's　gay,　and　bright,　and　free
　　　from care.

A summer season and a wounded heart—

    A young man's heart that suff'ring makes

        its moan—

Alas! that reason and true love should part;

    "Yield up, O love, thy crown and hearted

        throne."

And Cupid sneered, for Cupid's young no

    more,

    And in my face he puffed his cigarette;

"Drop sentiment,—it's such an awful bore;

    She has forgotten, he will soon forget!"

HE MADE US FREE.

S flame streams upward, so my longing
     thought
       Flies up with Thee
Thou God and Saviour, who hast truly
     wrought
Life out of death, and to us, loving, brought
A fresh, new world; and in Thy sweet chains
     caught,
       And made us free!

As hyacinths make way from out the dark,
       My soul awakes,
At thought of Thee, like sap beneath the bark;
As little violets in field and park
Rise to the trilling thrush and meadow-lark.
       New hope it takes.

As thou goest upward through the nameless
    space
        We call the sky,
Like jonquil perfume softly falls Thy grace;
It seems to touch and brighten every place,
Fresh flowers crown our wan and weary race,
        O Thou on high!

Hadst Thou not risen, there would be no joy
        Upon earth's sod;
Life would be still with us a wound or toy,
A cloud without the sun,—O Babe, O Boy,
O Man of Mother pure, with no alloy,
        O risen God!

Thou, God and King, didst "mingle in the
    game," *
        (Cease, all fears; cease!)
For love of us;—not to give Virgil's fame

* Tennyson.

Or Crœsus' wealth, not to make well the lame,

Or save the sinner from deservèd shame,

But for sweet Peace!

For peace, for joy;—not that the slave might
lie
In luxury,

Not that all woe from us should always fly,

Or golden crops with Syrian roses † vie

In every field; but in Thy peace to die

And rise,—be free!

† Virgil.

AT EASTER TIME.

THE sunset, like a flaming sword,
     Between our sight and Paradise.
     Offers its red fire to our eyes—
A symbol of earth's Lord.

The crocus shows above the ground
     Its glowing lamp of yellow flame,
     It seems a letter of the Name
Which choirs of angels sound.

An altar all this fair earth is,
     The Christian mind the priest,
     The greatest thinker or the least
Is acolyte of His.

For nature gives us what we bring,

    Not more, nor any less;

    The meaning of her varied dress

Must in our minds first spring.

Thus Easter gilds the opening year,

    Because Christ is our joy;

    The sunset brave, the crocus coy,

Reflect Him bright and clear.

Nature's a sphinx to those who know

    Not Resurrection time!

    We read her well; in every clime

Faith makes her meaning glow.

NARRATIVE POEMS

NARRATIVE POEMS.

THE FRIAR'S RUBY.

HE sea and the sky are the servants of God,
And the earth is his footstool, too;
Dark deeds may be done at a despot's nod,
God's servants will bring them to view.

He has hid his crime in the deep, deep sea:
Who has seen its stain on land?
But the sky knows all, and his hopes shall be
As false as words in the sand!

When Fra Gonsales in St. Francis' robe

Came to the peons in fair Mexico,

"Great Doctor" called they him; their

every woe

He found and cured with balsam and with
    probe.

And so they said: "A Spaniard can be
    good"—
    At first amazed.—"This Christian does
    not smite
    And goad us as the soldiers, nor does spite
Or malice gleam beneath his blessèd hood."

The peaceful Friar wrought for many a day
    Among the peons by the restless sea—
    The chopping Gulf—that in the land
    might be
An altar to the Truth, the Light, the Way.

His bronze-hued children worked Gonsales'
    will,
    And other friars came, and soldiers, few—

Sent by the King the Friar's will to do—
Came to a place where evil tongues were still.

And with them Castro Mendez—"Cruel Eye"
    The peons called him—wily captain he
    Of Andalusian Guards: the charity
Of Fra Gonsales saw no danger nigh.

Castro loved gold. "The pious monk's a fool!
    If he were not," he said, "I'd force these
        slaves
    To be *my* slaves; what though Spain's
        standard waves,
If men are but the toys of this priest's rule!"

Storm came on storm borne on the northern
        wind,
    And boats went down in darkness of the
        night.

" Oh! if to sea I could but cast a light!"
Oft sighed the Friar, for he loved his kind.

And in the season of these stormy blasts
    Gonsales' church was finished; high it
      rose
    The sea-wind facing—and the great God
      knows
How, poem-like, it had grown in tears and
      fasts!

While friars fasted, Castro cursed his fate,
    "O, for Pizarro's power to balk the
      priests—
    O, for a day of lavish gold and feasts
Luxurious and gay.—The priest wakes late!"

He heard the Friar calling on the name
    St. Antony, and saw him as he prayed.

Just then a peon entered and soft laid
A glowing ruby down, a rose of flame.

" 'T is yours, O Father! It came from the
        mine
        Called Wondrous, in the gorge by Inca's
        plain,
For which the hated soldiers sought in vain.
Take it, my Father; keep it, it is thine! "

Don Castro heard; beneath his knitted brow
        Shot out a serpent-flame of evil light,
        And with desire his lips and cheeks grew
        white.
"Go, gold," he said, "I shall have rubies
        now! "

Don Castro sneered as Fra Gonsales raised
        His hands to Antony, the loving saint,

And like the Antony that artists paint
Gonsales looked as his sweet Lord he praised.

Niched in the church-front stood the loving
        Maid,
    The Mother-Queen Immaculate as fair,
    Above her the rose-window, high in air;—
In it was put the ruby many-rayed.

By grace of the great Paduan, rich it glowed
    Through the dark, windy nights far out
        to sea,
    A lighthouse to the sailors; gratefully
Their prayers to Christ's sweet Mother nightly
        flowed.

The ruby of the window, red by day,
    But burning like a hundred fires by night,
    Until the Gulf with crimson was alight,

To seamen showed the safe and peaceful way.

Don Castro sought—the mine he could not
       gain,
    (St. Antony, mayhap, had hid the place).
    Bitter his heart and bitter looked his face;
How sad is he who seeks for gems in vain!

He grew to hate Gonsales and his love
    For "the slave-hearted peons"; holy rood
    To him was irksome as St. Francis' hood:
Who seeks for self can seldom look above.

The devil, in his soul, became more bold,—
    Don Castro dreamed of imps with jeweled
       eyes,
    Of serpents crimsoned in strong ruby
       dyes,
And waking cried, "My crimson soul is sold!"

One night he did the deed; the Friar knelt
    Beneath the ruby and Our Lady's
        shrine—

    "St. Antony!"—a gasp—a poniard's
        shine:
Don Castro, mounted high, no sorrow felt.

Beneath the window lay a crimson pool,
    And on the sea there shone no crimson fire;
    Don Castro, stained with red, had his
        desire,
He held the ruby—he the devil's fool!

The night was lightless, twice unsteadily
    Don Castro wavered, then he falling
        caught
    The ruby to his heart—the good he
        sought
Fell with him to the bottom of the sea.

At Vera Cruz this simple tale is told,
    And near its coast the sea at eve is red
    With light of the great ruby in its bed
Beneath the waves, in false Don Castro's hold.

The Friar's Love still lives: Love never dies;
    For still the sea in storms is crimson-lit,
    Where stood Our Lady's church; no
        pilot's wit
Is now at fault; the white sail homeward flies.

He has hid his crime in the deep, deep sea:
    Who has seen its stain on land?
But the sky knows all, and his hopes shall be
    As false as words in the sand.

The sea and the sky are God's warders true,
    Each whispers to each all day,
The lips of the gray and the ear of the blue
    Are telling and hearing alway.

DOÑA INEZ.

(SUGGESTED BY DORÉ'S "SPANISH BEGGARS.")

HROUGH the widest street in Cadiz
    Doña Inez rode one day,
Clad in costly silk and laces,
    In a group of friends as gay.

Near the portals of a convent—
    From the Moors just lately won—
Sat a crowd of dark-skinned beggars
    Basking in the pleasant sun;
One an old man—he a Christian
    Blind to all the outward light—
Told his black beads, praying softly
    For all poor souls still in night.

"I am but a Moorish beggar,"
    Said a woman with a child;

" I am but a Moorish beggar,

> And the Moors are fierce and wild.

You may *talk* of Christian goodness—

> Christian Faith and Charity,

But *I'll* never be a Christian

> 'Till some proof of these I see.

Christians are as proud and haughty

> As the proudest Moor of all;

And they hate the men that hate them

> With a hate like bitter gall."

" You judge rashly, O my sister,

> In the words you speak to me."

" I would be a Christian, blind man:

> Show me Christian charity!

" Lo! here comes proud Doña Inez,

> Very rich and fair to see;

I am but a Moorish beggar,

> Will the lady come to me?

No! she will not, for she hateth
    All the children of the Moor.
If she come, I tell you, blind man,
    I will kneel, and Christ adore!"

Passing was the Lady Inez
    When the dark group met her eye,
And she leant from out her litter
    Smiling on them tenderly.
"They are poor, they are God's children,"
    Said a voice within her soul,
And she lightly from her litter
    Stepped to give the beggars dole.

Sneered, and laughed, and laughing, won-
    dered
    All the other ladies gay;
And the Lady Inez knew not
    She had saved a soul that day.

JEAN RENAUD.

(GERARD DE NERVAL.)

HEN Jean Renaud came home from
the war,

His body and mind were sick and sore.

"Good-day, my mother." "Good-day, my
son;

Your little child's life has just begun."

"Arrange, my mother, the great white bed,

That I may lie down and rest my head;

But make no noise, my mother, for fear

My wife on her couch of pain may hear."

And when the old hamlet clock had tolled

The midnight hour, the death-angel rolled

Away the stone from the cave of life,

And Jean Renaud passed from sin and strife.

"Mother, dear mother," his poor wife said,

"Why do they sing as if one were dead?"

"Daughter, dear daughter, 't is but a crowd

That passes us by, chanting aloud."

"But, mother, my dear, why weep you so?

I see the tears as they shine and flow."

"Alas! the sad truth I cannot hide,

'T is our own poor Jean who has just died."

"O mother, say to the sexton, who

Digs in the earth, that a grave for two

Must be made so very wide and deep

That my husband, I, and our child may sleep."

THE BARD'S STORY.

[The Prince of this legend was the husband of Ethna, who, with her sister Fidalma, also a Princess of Meath, saw St. Patrick celebrating Mass one morning by a river. They were attracted by the sight; he answered their questions and baptized them.]

OVE makes man's life a glory; Hate, a hell;

A warning to all warriors, this I tell:

Strongest of the Fini, he, the Prince, alone

Knelt by the river, sad, and made his moan.

His lands were wide, his people staunch and
    true,

And in his palace four fair children grew.

His wife was Ethna, Princess mild of Meath,

Graceful and tall—a lily in its sheath.

The Mass was said each day beneath his roof,

And evil from his household held aloof.

And he had seen great Patrick when he came,

At Paschal time, and lighted Christian flame.

And he had seen the saint make poison good

By words of prayer, while hatred near him
　　　stood.

And only in defense of clan and life,

Since he had learned of Christ, had he made
　　　strife.

But though his cattle grazed in richest green,

Black spots and red spots by the river's sheen;

And though his bards his prowess daily sang,

His moans beside the reedy river rang

At fall of night—some piercing loud and
　　　shrill,

Others that brought to hearers death-like
　　　chill.

"*Forgive, forgive!*" he murmured; "*oh! forgive!*

How can I bear my load of sin and live?

Oh! words of fire you spoke, great Patrick, Saint,

Ere the clear stream had washed from me sin's

taint.

'Even Red Conn, the slayer of your kin,

Forgive, forgive, if you would Heaven win.'

'*He slew my men.*' 'Forgive,' the Saint replied,

'Though through his wrath your clansmen
oft have died.'

'Forgive,' he said. '*He laughed my threats to*
scorn!'

'Forgive, forgive! and win eternal morn.'

'Forgive Red Conn, and hurt him not, I pray;

Your sister's son is he. Forgive, I say!'

'*Let me but fight for Christ with sword and*
brand—'

'Thou canst not fight thy sin with carnal
     hand!'
And then I promised, and the water flowed,
And all my heart with love of Patrick glowed.

Conn came not near me; hid he dark and deep
In marsh and bog where strange, wild crea-
     tures sleep.
Once, when I thought of clansmen cold and
     dead,
Killed by his hand ere he to bogs had fled,

My wrath awoke, but dying soon in peace,
It to my better musings gave release.
Peace made me proud. One day I chased
     the deer,
And found my enemy crouched low in fear

Among the fern. I made a bound at him;
He fled, not fighting, to this river's brim.

Pale, worn, he was; my hatred quick awoke,
But in my heart the voice of Patrick spoke.

'Forgive, forgive!' I heard the whisper run
All through the reeds. 'Remember Mary's
    Son.'
I listened not: I drove Conn to his knee;
His eyes were like a deer's in agony.

My brain was drunk with rage, my blood was
    fire,
His death—the death of Conn was my desire.
His eyes were all that spoke; the whispering
    leaves
Said, 'Oh! forgive; great Patrick for you
    grieves.'

I struck him down, and then looked in his
    face.
O Christ! O God! how I did lose Thy grace!

I saw his face! 'T was Conn's no more! O
    sight!
Wouldst Thou hadst shriveled me, O Lord
    of light!

I saw His face, as He is on the cross!
There He lay prone upon the sodden moss.
The blood was His, not Conn's, that reddened
    all
The little shallows where the reeds grew tall."

    *   *   *   *   *   **

And, as the world shall last, the legends say,
Sweet Ethna's husband moans his life away.
Among the reeds his sighing all may hear;
And may it such grace-losing make us fear!

For Love makes life a glory; Hate is vain,
Except to wound our Saviour's heart again.

A SWEDISH LEGEND.

"THOU wilt be mine!" the Swedish
monarch sighed.

"No; never thine!" the fair Christine replied.

"Thou hast a queen—a good and lovely
bride."

"But thou shalt have bright robes and laces
old,

And thou shalt wear a dazzling crown of gold,

And thou shalt half of all my kingdom hold!"

"My soul is dearer than thy garments bright;

I love not flowers plucked in guilt's dark
night;

I fear the wrong, I love God's holy right."

"Thou shalt be mine, or die in torture dire,

Thou shalt not die by water or by fire,

My love was life, now death is my desire."

And in a cask, strong-spiked with points of
        steel,

Men place the maiden, and then roughly wheel

The cask along by blow of fist and heel.

Ah, she is dead, with blood upon her brow;

Three angels with white wings before her
        bow

And bear her up,—her pain is rapture now.

A BALLAD OF ISCANDER-BEG.

I.

"ST. MICHAEL stands upon my right,
    Therefore I have no fear;
When he shall cease his holy fight
    My end will then be near."
Thus spake the brave George Castriot
Albania's Christian knight,
Who once with Moslems cast his lot,
(With those who love our Jesu not).

They called him by another name—
    The hateful Moslem crew! —
Iscander-Beg! They knew his fame,
    And deep that fame they rue.

To-day, beside the Golden Horn,

Full many a Moslem dame

Most sore affrights her latest born

With that bright name that Christians mourn.

His father was a noble good,

    His mother, sweet and fair,

Who loved our Jesu's holy rood

    And breathed forth many a prayer

For those who with the infidel

In need of Christian solace stood,

And in their sins were forced to dwell

(Her prayers, O Castriot, served thee well!).

The Turkish hordes swept down one day,

    Ferocious and armed well,

Four little boys that were at play

    A hostage to them fell;

For Christians could not hold their own—

They were the Moslem's prey.

Three of them had to Heaven flown

Before the fourth was fully grown.

Albania's blood flowed swift and true

    Within his princely veins;

The Sultan learned to know it, too,

    And kept in golden chains

The soul of him that was Christ's child,

Baptized as he knew well;

But conscience-stifled, soul-beguiled,

His heart and strength grew fierce and wild.

" Weak are the corselets you have brought! "

    The fearful Sultan said

Unto the armorers, who wrought

    Strong shields for heart and head.

"My bold Albanian's naked skin,

His arms when clothed with naught,

Will let no arrow enter in;

To him your thickest steel is thin.

Hail, Alexander,* lord and prince!"
    The fearful Sultan cried,
Not dreaming that his hosts would wince
    Before that name of pride.
Iscander-Beg is Castriot,
(How deep his great sword dints!)
Though for a time he cast his lot
With those who loved our Jesu not.

II.

He reveled with the Moslem swine,
    Pierced many a true man's heart;
He spilled our Christian blood like wine,
    And fought with skillful art;
But the Good Shepherd sought for him,
From him God would not part,
For "Salve" ('twas his childish hymn)
Stopped many a sinful thought and whim.

*Iscander-Beg—Lord Alexander.

For childish thoughts are lifetime's dreams
  Within us unto death,
They come upon us when pain seems
  To stop our very breath.
And so Iscander-Beg, the strong,
At least the legend saith,
Was led by childish thoughts along
By music of the " Salve " song.

And mothers' prayers work wonders strange,
  They never are in vain;
No earthly power can check their range,
  No heavenly will.   'T is plain
Christ's Mother loves all mothers well,
Can *She* be deaf to mothers' pain?
So 'Scander-Beg, an infidel,
Apostate came from Moslem hell.

There shone a day for Christian lands,
  A wonder-working day,

When Castriot looked at his hands,

    All soiled with bloody clay:

"My soul's like this, God's mark is there,

No sin can hide that mark away!

My sins are scarlet; can I dare

To ask the Christ to make me fair?"

A mother's prayers all battles win!

    He left his worthless gold,

He cast aside the nets of sin

    That chained him in their hold.

He tore away the crescent moon

Which fast was growing (Moslems told

How it would swing o'er Europe soon).

It waned!—this was a mother's boon.

"Iscander-Beg!" he cried, "to hell

    I cast that title vile;

I spit upon thee, infidel;

    At all thy honors false, I smile.

Poor as a monk, I choose the cross;

Ah! never shall vain things beguile

Me to the loving of base dross;

These honors to the fiends I toss!"

We know the rest: he saved the world,

 Our world, from Moslems' rule,

And on their running ranks he hurled

 (This man who had been Moslems' tool!)

His mighty strength.   Brave Castriot

Became a child in Jesu's school;

Knelt weeping that he cast his lot

With those who loved our Lady not.

Oh! thoughts of childhood do not die

 Like thoughts of man and youth;

They change not like an April sky

 They live in lies or truth,

And, be they false or be they true,

They work us good or ruth;

And well George Castriot's mother knew
That Jesu grants when mothers sue.

"St. Michael stands upon my right,
    My own right arm I bare;
While he is with me in the fight,
    I need no armor there.
My sword, best tempered blade of all,
Will cleave a yielding hair!
But if Lord Jesu will, I fall—
Maria! hear a sinner's call!"

SONNETS

PERPETUAL YOUTH.

IS said there is a fount in Flower
Land,—
De Leon found it,—where Old Age away
Throws weary mind and heart, and fresh as day
Springs from the dark and joins Aurora's band:
This tale, transformed by some skilled trou-
vère's wand
From the old myth in a Greek poet's lay,
Rests on no truth. Change bodies as Time
may,
Souls do not change though heavy be his hand.
Who of us needs this fount ? What soul is old ?

Age is a mask,—in heart we grow more young,

For in our winters we talk most of spring;

And as we near, slow-tottering, God's safe fold,

Youth's loved ones gather nearer;—though among

The seeming dead, youth's songs more clear they sing.

OF ONE WE LOVE OR HATE.

IN old Assisi, Francis loved so well

　His Lady Poverty, that to his heart

He pressed her heart, nor felt the deadly smart

From lips of frost, nor saw the fire of hell

From lurid eyes that fevered Dante's cell,

And parches souls who, hating, feel her dart.

He chose her, and he dwelt with her apart.

The two were one, illumined through Love's

　　spell:

He loved her, and she glowed, a lambent star;

He loved her, and the birds came at his call—

Her frosts were pearls, her face was fair to see.

He sang his lady's praises near and far,

He saw our world as Adam ere the Fall—

So Love transfigures even Poverty.

THEOCRITUS.

DAPHNIS is mute, and hidden nymphs
    complain,
And mourning mingles with their fountains'
    song;
Shepherds contend no more, as all day long
They watch their sheep on the wide, cyprus-
    plain;
The master-voice is silent, songs are vain;
Blithe Pan is dead, and tales of ancient wrong
Done by the gods, when gods and men were
    strong,
Chanted to reeded pipes, no prize can gain.
O sweetest singer of the olden days,
In dusty books your idyls rare seem dead;

The gods are gone, but poets never die;

Though men may turn their ears to newer lays,

Sicilian nightingales enrapturèd

Caught all your songs, and nightly thrill the

sky.

MAURICE DE GUÉRIN.

THE old wine filled him, and he saw, with eyes
Anoint of Nature, fauns and dryads fair
Unseen by others; to him maidenhair
And waxen lilacs, and those birds that rise
A-sudden from tall reeds at slight surprise,
Brought charmèd thoughts; and in earth everywhere
He, like sad Jaques, found a music rare
As that of Syrinx to old Grecians wise.
A pagan heart, a Christian soul had he,
He followed Christ, yet for dead Pan he sighed,
Till earth and heaven met within his breast;
As if Theocritus in Sicily
Had come upon the Figure crucified
And lost his gods in deep, Christ-given rest.

JESSICA.

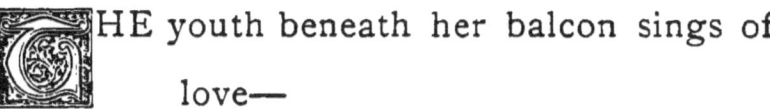HE youth beneath her balcon sings of
love—

Old Shylock's gone: "O Jessica, come thou

Unto this heart which in one fervent vow

Has burned its flesh and blood!" The
moments move

As days in Eden; she goes, like a dove,

From great St. Mark's at Venice, to endow

Her lover with her life.   The rosy Now

Seems Heaven itself, and he the Lord thereof.

But love is rainbow-tinted, and as short

As is the life of rainbows. "Mine? Oh, nay!"

Say'st thou, fair Jessica, who maketh sport

Of that old Jew, thy father?   In love's court

Thou dost eat lotus, but old lovers say

To love's own chamber memories oft resort.

A NIGHT IN JUNE.

I.

RICH is the scent of clover in the air,
    And from the woodbine, moonlight
        and the dew
Draw finer essence than the daylight knew;
Low murmurs and an incense everywhere!
Who spoke?   Ah! surely in the garden there
A subtile sound came from the purple crew
That mount wistaria masts, and there's a clue
Of some strange meaning in the rose-scent rare:
Silence itself has voice in these June nights—
Who spoke? Why, all the air is full of speech
Of God's own choir, all singing various parts;

Be quiet and listen: hear—the very lights

In yonder town, the waving of the beech,

The maples' shades,—cry of the Heart of

hearts!

II.

On such a night spoke raptured Juliet

From out the balcon; and young Rosalind,

Wandered in Arden like the April wind;

And Jessica the bold Lorenzo met;

And Perdita her silvered lilies set

In some quaint vase, to scent the Prince's mind

With thoughts of her; and then did Jaques find

Sad tales, and from them bitter sayings get.

To all of these the silence sang their thought;

To all of these it gave their thought new grace:

Soprano of the lily, roses' lone

And passionate contralto, oak boughs' bass—

All sing the thought we bring them, be it
        fraught
With the sad love of lovers, or God's own.

III.

This sweetness and this silence fill my soul
With longing and dull pain, that seem to
        break
Some cord within my heart, and sudden take
Life out of life; and then there sounds the roll
Of wheels upon the road, the distant toll
Of bells within the town: these rude things
        make
Life wake to life; and all the longings shake
Their airy wings,—swift fly the pain and dole.
Again the silence and the mute sounds sweet
Begin their speaking; I alone am still
What are you singing, O you starry flowers

Upon the jasmine ?—"Void and incomplete."

And you, clematis ?—"Void the joys that fill

The heart of love until His Heart is ours."

IV.

O choir of silence, without noise of word!

A human voice would break the mystic spell

Of wavering shades and sounds; the lily bell

Here at my feet sings melodies unheard;

And clearer than the voice of any bird,—

Yes, even than that lark which loves so well,

Hid in the hedges, all the world to tell

In trill and triple notes that May has stirred.

"O Love complete!" soft sings the mignonette;

"O Heart of All!" deep sighs the red, red
rose;

"O Heart of Christ!" the lily voices meet

In fugue on fugue; and from the flag-edged,
wet,

Lush borders of the lake, the night wind blows

The tenor of the reeds—" Love, love complete!"

THE JOY-BRINGER.

I.

OT when old Bion's idyls sweet were
   sung,

Or when fine Horace scorned the vulgar herd,

And praised his frugal fare—each chosen word

Writ where full skins of rare Falernian hung

Above a table with rich garlands flung

By Roman slaves; not when the dancer stirred

The air of spring, like swaying wave or bird,

Was there true joy the tribes of men among!

These idyls and these odes hide sadness deep

And canker worms despite the shining gold

We gild them with; their lucent music flows

To noble words at times, but words of sleep,

But words of dreaming; life was not Life of

     old,—

It came to earth when God the Son arose!

II.

The fair façade, the carved acanthus leaf,

The sparkling sea where clearest blue meets

     blue,

The piled-up roses, steeped in silver dew

Upon the marble tiles, the white-robed chief

Of some great group of men seeks cool relief

Upon a galley hung with every hue

That glads the eye, while violets slave girls

     strew

To cithern-sounds;—this picture artists drew:

And, moved, our poets cry for the dead Pan;

Turn from the rood and sing the fluted reed,—

"Arcadia, O Arcadia, come again!"

A cry of fools—a cry unworthy man

Who was a sodden thing before the Deed

Of Love Divine turned blinded slaves to men!

CONSOLATION.

I.

THE swift years pass, fast flies the snow,
    Fast blow the gusts of autumn time,
Fast grows the summer from its prime,
Fast the world-currents ebb and flow,
Comes death, goes life, and like the glow
Of poet's thoughts in poet's rhyme
That raise us to a golden clime,
Illusions soothe us as we go:
We are but children,—God is great!
In face of death we could not live,
Were there no castles in the clouds,
No earthly hopes that hearts elate,
No daily joys His dear hands give,
No flowers to hide the sombre shrouds.

New days! new friends—we love them all!

God gives new sunlight each new day,

And when the older pass away,

He throws some blossoms on death's pall,—

He puts fresh garlands on the wall

That hides from us the holy ray,—

The Blessed Vision that alway

Will shine for those who hear His call:

Which are the deeper,—smiles or prayers?

Why chide us, if we laugh to-day

With newer friends, when hearts are cold

That once knew all our joys and cares?

No man is false, who, true, can say

"Smiles for the new, prayers for the old!"

RAPHAEL.

TEEPED in the glow and glory of old
    Rome—

So old, so young, in life, and death, and art—

His pictures shine, so near to Truth's great
    heart,

That through the ages Truth has in her home

The brightest stars in her celestial dome

Kept them alive; and will, till time is done,

Fill them with stronger light than fire or sun.

Great Prince of Painters! laurel wreathes his
    name;

The world may babble,—she's an ancient
    dame!

And say his life and art held much of clay,

Reproaching him; yet saints fell on their way.

If sin repented be a blot on fame,

His fame is fameless, though he reached fame's

goal,

And left us glory shining from his soul.

FRA ANGELICO.

ART is true art when art to God is true,

   And only then: to copy Nature's work

Without the chains that run the whole world

      through

Gives us the eye without the lights that lurk

In its clear depths: no soul, no truth is there.

Oh, praise your Rubens and his fleshly brush!

Oh, love your Titian and his carnal air!

Give me the trilling of a pure-toned thrush,

And take your crimson parrots. Artist—saint!

O Fra Angelico, your brush was dyed

In hues of opal, not in vulgar paint;

You showed to us pure joys for which you

      sighed.

Your heart was in your work, you never
feigned:

You left us here the Paradise you gained!

COLUMBUS THE WORLD-GIVER.

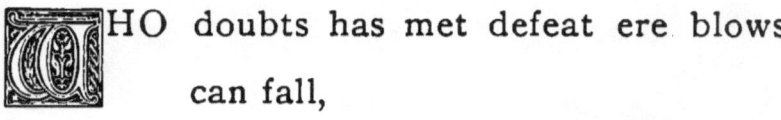

WHO doubts has met defeat ere blows
    can fall,
Who doubts must die with no palm in his hand;
Who doubts shall never be of that high band
Which clearly answer—Present! to Death's
    call;
For Faith is life, and, though a funeral pall
Veil our fair Hope, and on our promised land
A mist malignant hang, if Faith but stand
Among our ruins we shall conquer all.

O faithful soul, that knew no doubting low.
O Faith incarnate, lit by Hope's strong flame,
And led by Faith's own cross to dare all ill
And find our world!—but more than this we
    owe

To thy true heart; thy pure and glorious name

Is one clear trumpet call to Faith and Will.

CERVANTES.

HERE was a time when books of chiv-
   alry
Were full of monster-men and dragons great;
When Amadis of Gaul and his fair mate
Were bound in love against all rivalry;
When he who strove a faithful knight to be
Must lengthened vigils keep and, longing, wait
And also fight until he stood, elate,
O'er giants and dragons in proud victory.

Then came Quixote, peerless gentleman,
Who put the dragons and the giants to flight,
And turned the world from knights all amor-
   ous;
Then through the world the rippled laughter
   ran

When Sancho came. No shadows are the
knight
And clown our great Cervantes made for us.

FREDERIC OZANAM.

 SOUL alight with purest flame of love,
    A heart aglow with sweetest charity,
A mind all filled—and this is rarity—
With even·balanced thoughts, his eyes above,
Yet saw the earth in its dread verity;
For is't not true that some who Heaven see
Cast down no looks upon the shadows of
This shadowed world? A serpent, yet a dove,
He read the world and, seeking, found the clue
To all the secrets of our troubled time,
And from the past drew other secrets down;
He placed, 'mid Dante's bays, a diamond true
Of purest water; and in every clime
Prayers of God's poor add gems to his bright
    crown.

AT THE END OF AUTUMN.

LOST ! all the flush of roses and of skies
    That change at morning to the red of
    eve,
O'er clover-waves that in soft meadows heave
In foam of blossoms with white-fringèd eyes—
The changing glamour that the sun fays leave,
The snow of summer that on green sward lies
When roses faint and all their spells unweave
In vale and coppice, ere the autumn flies!

Ah, naught is left to me but winter days,
For all my summer has been lost to me
Amid dull drudging in the toil of trade.
Lost gold of grain fields, green of country
    ways—

A dream!—my dream! for one whole day of
    ye
I'd risk all gold of men, and be well paid!

TRUE LOVE.

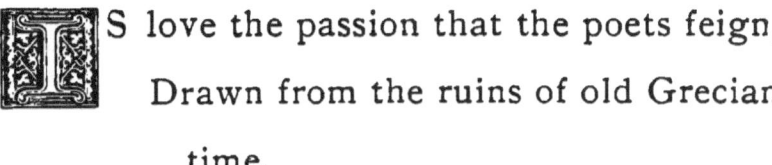S love the passion that the poets feign,
Drawn from the ruins of old Grecian
time,
Born of the Hermæ and all earthly slime,
And tricked by troubadours in trappings vain
Of flowers fantastic, like a Hindoo fane,
Or the long meter of an antique rhyme
Dancing in dactyls? Is love, then, a crime—
A rosy day's eternity of pain?

If we love God, we know what loving is;
For love is God's: He sent it to the earth,
Half-human, half-divine, all glorious—
Half-human, half-divine, but wholly His;
Not loving God, we know not true love's worth,
We taste not the great gift He gave for us.

THE CHRYSALIS OF A BOOKWORM.

READ, O friend, no pages of old lore,
Which I loved well, and yet the fly-
ing days,
That softly passed as wind through green
spring ways
And left a perfume, swift fly as of yore,
Though in clear Plato's stream I look no more,
Neither with Moschus sing Sicilian lays,
Nor with bold Dante wander in amaze,
Nor see our Will the Golden Age restore.
I read a book to which old books are new,
And new books old.   A living book is mine—
In age, three years: in it I read no lies;
In it to myriad truths I find the clue—

A tender, little child; but I divine

Thoughts high as Dante's in her clear blue

      eyes.

THE AFTER THOUGHT.

HY is it that our life seems full of
      wrong?

That even poets, who are human birds,

Set saddest music to the saddest words,

And mingle sighs and tears in all their song?

For Chaucer's marguerites still bloom along

Our rustic fences, herdsmen and their herds

Know Shakespeare's cookoo-cups, and the
      new curds

Are hard and white, and violet-scent is strong:

'Tis not because the gods are silent all,

For in Siena the Brigata held

Their revels, and joy's golden badges wore,—

So sayeth sweet Folgore,—carnival

Reigned blithe and jocund;—Giant Thought
    has felled
The gay Page Laughter: there is mirth no
    more.

BY RIGHT DIVINE.

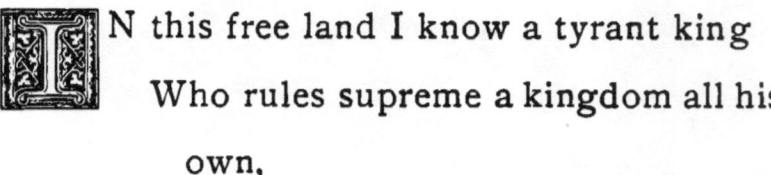N this free land I know a tyrant king
    Who rules supreme a kingdom all his
        own,
Who reigns supreme by right divine alone,
Who governs slaves that always cringe and
        sing,—
"He walks! He talks!" in most admiring
        tone;
They quail with fear if he but make a moan,
And wild confusion comes if he but fling
Away his scepter—coral, jingling thing!
He is a king, though loving anarchy,
A tyrant king, whom our fond land obeys,
A tyrant king, yet scarce a mimic man;

And this whole land is bound in monarchy,

All mother-hearts some little ruler sways,

If harder fathers be republican.

ON MEADOWS GREEN.

HEN the first blush and bloom of life
have fled,

And on the summit of youth's mound we stand,

And youth to manhood gladly gives his hand,

And then quick dies, and manhood in his stead

Shows us a mist that hides an unknown land,

By wild, chill breezes are our faces fanned:

The world before us!—and no longer red,

Nor glowing with fair hope, for youth is dead.

A mist all gray is drawn before the world—

This great wide life!   To fight life all alone

Is now our lot; yet other men have seen

The same vague foe; and patient souls have
hurled

Their fear away, and, going, made no moan,

To find the mist God's rain on meadows green.

ILLUSION.

(AFTER A SONNET BY SAINTE-BEUVE.)

INTO the dimness of a chamber closed,
   Curtained with care and full of slum-
      b'rous rest,
A ray of light came, slopèd from the west,
To the small cradle where a child reposed—
A dainty cradle, laced and satin-rosed
By mother's hand, and in its fairy nest
The child soft slumbered, by the angels blest—
Near it lay Mouser, white-furred and pink-
      nosed:
The cat was motionless as if of clay,
Until the gold ray moved upon the floor
O'er crimson carpet in its wanton game,—

Then all a-sudden Mouser saw the ray

And chased it till it vanished evermore:

Ah, sleeping child, thus *we* chase wealth and

    fame!

NOVEMBER.

HE crimson and the russet and the
    gold,
The palest green that gives a hint of spring,
And nameless colors that swift breezes fling
From waving trees: tall dahlias crisped by cold
Vie with the sunrise, as some men when old
Are brightest, or as swans, when dying, sing,
Or a sweet strain the fickle zephyrs bring
Stopped short before its burden is all told.
O fair November, lesson us, we pray;
O sweet, sad season, teach us ere you go;
O teach us, ere your mellow lights have passed,
The secret in the fading of your day;
That when life's end approaches, we may know
The way to make our fairest, brightest, LAST!

LEGENDS OF THE FLOWERS.

OF FLOWERS.

HERE were no roses till the first child
     died,

No violets, nor balmy-breathed heart's-ease,

No heliotrope, nor buds so dear to bees,

The honey-hearted suckle, no gold-eyed

And lowly dandelion, nor, stretching wide,

Clover and cowslip-cups, like rival seas,

Meeting and parting as the young spring breeze

Runs giddy races playing seek and hide:

For all flowers died when Eve left Paradise;

And all the world was flowerless awhile,

Until a little child was laid in earth;

Then from its grave grew violets for its eyes,

And from its lips rose-petals for its smile,

And so all flowers from that child's death
took birth.

I.

THE CHILD.

N the late winter, when the breath of
spring
Had almost softened the great fields of snow,
A mother died, and, wandering to and fro,
Her sad child sought her—frightened little
thing!—
Through the drear woodland, as on timid wing
A young bird flutters; in the bushes low
It sunk in sleep, thus losing all its woe,
With smiling lips her dear name murmuring:
No loving arms were there to hold it fast,
There were no kisses for it warm and sweet,
But snowflakes, pitying, fell like frozen tears.

Then said its angel, " Snowflakes, ye shall last

Beyond the life of snowflakes; at Spring's feet

Bloom ye as flowers through all the coming
years!"

II.

MARGARET.

SHAMED before the world a woman
stood

Near a great church, where lovely statues line

The vaulted chapels; if tears be a sign

Of sorrow, she was sorrowing; her hood

Showed golden hair astray that never could,

Even in sin, forget its young design

To curl like tendrils of a summer vine.

From out the church passed women sternly
good;

Upon her fevered brow was laid no hand,

Though Christ had blessed her sister Magda-
 len;

She wept and prayed, yet scornful words were
 said;

But soon soft snowflakes, falling o'er the land,

Soothed her hot brow: her angel spoke, "*These*,
 then,

Shall bloom as flowers when ye lie cold and
 dead."

III.

A ROMAUNT OF THE ROSE.

 FAIRER light than ever since has
 shone,

Fell on that garden where Queen Eve's sweet
 bower

Was hid in roses and the jasmine flower,

Curtained with eglantine, and overrun

With morning-glories glowing in the sun
Late into noon, unheeding of the hour
When now they close; these were our mother's
    dower!
She lived and loved amid all flowers, save one.
There was no red rose in the garden wide
Of all her world, until its mistress went
From out its gates with roses in her hand,
Spoil of past joys; then, like a new-made bride,

She redly blushed, and that first blush has lent
The rose its color over all our land.

THE HEART.

OW red it burns within yon crimson
        rose!

Deeper than fire in rubies is its hue

Of brightest blood, which, shed for me and you,

From that dear Heart has flowed, forever flows.

In waving sprays of buds, carved mountain
        snows,

I see *her* heart, forever pure and true,—

The Virgin's heart!—and in the morning dew

The tears of joy she shed when her great woes

Were lost in Heaven: and all June things speak,

From ambient perfume in the sunlit air

To trembling stalklets tipped by clover bloom,

Of Christ, His Mother, and the Heart we seek

Through tangled roads and by-ways foul or
fair,

The Heart that cheers us in the deepest gloom.

ORDER.

(FROM THE ITALIAN OF ST. FRANCIS D'ASSISI.)

Our Lord Speaks:

ND though I fill thy heart with warm-
est love,

Yet in true order must thy heart love me;

For without order can no virtue be.

By thine own virtue, then, I, from above

Stand in thy soul; and so, most earnestly,

Must love from turmoil be kept wholly free.

The life of fruitful trees, the seasons of

The circling year, move gently as a dove.

I measured all the things upon the earth;

Love ordered them, and order kept them fair,

And love to order must be truly wed.

O soul, why all this heat of little worth?

Why cast out order with no thought or care?

For by love's warmth must love be governèd.

SAINT TERESA TO OUR LORD.

 DO not love Thee for the joy, O Lord,
Which Thou hast promised souls who
love Thee well;
I do not fear Thee for the fires of hell
Which burn for those whose right to Thy
reward
Is lost by sin; but, with the whole accord
Of mind, and soul, and longing heart as well,
I love Thee for the time when Thou didst dwell
Scorned on the earth, mocked by a faithless
horde:
Were there no Heaven, I would love Thee still.
I love Thee for Thy cross, Thy thorn-crowned
Head;

For Thy dread Passion, Lord, I love Thee best;

And though in firmest hope I wait thy will,

Compared with love, my strongest hope is dead;

For, without hope, in love I'd, trusting, rest!

TROUBLED SOULS.

O seek true rest and peace in wilds
　　away,

It is not strange that men have fled the world

From all the storm and strife perpetual hurled

At the fair form of silence all the day;

For day and night do good and evil sway

In close-knit fight, as when the Titans twirled

And twisted in fierce combat: never furled

Is Satan's flag, blood-reddened in hell's ray.

And though Thy cross, dear Christ, shines
　　　　ever bright,

And Thy sweet Mother downward bends her
　　　　gaze,

And Thy high saints own us in brotherhood,—

Our souls are troubled, the world's wrong
  seems right,
Our sight is dim, we falter in the maze;
For all our evil seems so near our good.

PEACE.

EACE, not of earth, I ask of Thee, O
    God,

Peace, not in death, and yet Thy will be done;

I would not die until my soul has won

Some little grace: a barren, withered sod

My life has been,—now touch me with Thy rod,

That I may blossom, as in summer sun

Thy flowers open; pray Thee give me one

Sweet touch of peace, for I am but a clod.

I know that Thou art all and I am naught,

Yet I would show my new-found love for Thee

By days all filled with striving for thy grace.

Peace, peace, O peace! the peace which Thou
    hast bought

With Precious Blood for us, O give it me,

Dear Lamb of God, that I may see Thy face!

A QUESTION.

ROM thy whole life take all the sweet-
  est days
Of earthly joy; take love before it cools;
Take words far-brought by all the learnèd
  schools
Since man first thought; then take the bright-
  est rays
Which poets limnèd with their rose-flushed
  tools;
Take heart-wrung music chastened with strict
  rules
Of greatest masters; and in all thy ways
Find things that make men only pleasure's
  fools.

Take these; beside them lay one heart-felt
     prayer;
Take these; beside them lay one little deed—
One simple act done for the great Christ-
     Heart—
And all earth's fairest toys like graspless air
To it will be; this being, then what need
To strive for things that will, with time,
     depart?

THE ANSWER.

ET me forget the world—all, all, but
Thee;

Let my whole soul arise as smoke from fire

In praise of Thee; let only one desire

Fill my whole heart—that through eternity,

Forever and forever, I may be

As incense ever rising to the Sire,

The Son, and Spirit; may I never tire

Of praising thus the glorious Trinity!

Poor soul, poor soul, such earthliness hast thou!

The world's thyself, thou canst not flee from it;

Thy prayers are selfish when thou prayest best,

Thy love is little, and thy warmest vow

As charred wood moistened, the fire free from

it;

Thou lackest much, but Christ will give the

rest.

WE CONQUER GOD.

WORLD, great world, now thou art all my own,

In the deep silence of my soul I stay

The current of thy life, though the wild day

Surges around me, I am all alone;—

Millions of voices rise, yet my weak tone

Is heard by Him who is the Light, the Way,

All Life, all Truth, the center of Love's ray;

Clamor, O Earth, the Great God hears my moan!

Prayer is the talisman that gives us all,

We conquer God by force of His own love,

He gives us all; when prostrate we implore—

The Saints must listen; prayers pierce Heaven's
    wall;
The humblest soul on earth, when mindful of
Christ's promise, is the greatest conqueror.

AFTER LENT.

OW the drear storm is past, the snow is
      gone,
And from the brown earth peeps the violet,
And from the west, where late the dim sun set
In winter clouds with weak rays, pale and wan,
Comes light reflected of a newer dawn;
Dark days have passed since the sad Mother
      met
The sweet Saint John, with her dark garments
      wet
With precious blood shed by the Holy One:

Light in the East!—Light in the East! The sun
Up-blazes in his splendor from the gloom.

Light in the East!—and all the doubt is past,

And all earth's beauty buds,—the risen One

Has taken from our race the seal of doom,—

Sweet peace has come,—and we are free at last!

"RESURREXIT SICUT DIXIT."

"AND He has risen!" O my God, my Lord,

When shall I cease to pierce Thy heart with
woe?

For all my life I've wandered to and fro

From sin to sin, and Thou hast kept strict
ward

And watch upon me, staying Thy dread sword

Of justice o'er me.   Even now I know,

Though I have washed where the clear waters
flow

From out Thy rock, my heart is with a cord

Bound fast to sin. "And He is Christ indeed!"

And all His brightness makes me feel my sin;

For as He brightens, I grow darker still—

A spot upon Christ's sun; yet, in my need

For me He's risen!   I will enter in

His joyful heart, and wait His holy will!

THE LESSON OF THE SEASON.

HAT comfort now, when summer days
          have fled,

Have you, O heart, that in the sunshine basked?

Have ye, O hands, that held all that was asked?

For all your fruits and flowers lie frosted, dead.

You did not dream amid the roses red,

Gold-hearted, scented, which your green
          bowers masked,

That cold would come, and with it wild winds
          tasked

To tear away the garlands from your head.

O lover of red roses and red wine,

O scorner of Christ's Blood, to whom a prayer

Brought thoughts of dying, shudders, and
  vague fear,
Will dreams of pleasure and past joys of thine
Make dreary winter hours more bright and fair
Amid your dust and ashes? Death is here.

GOLDEN NOON.

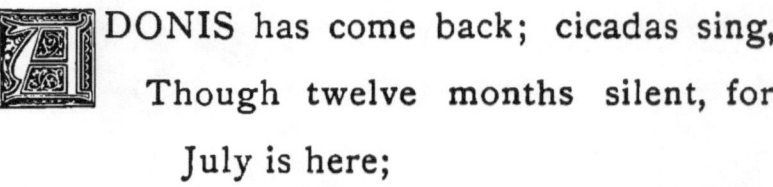DONIS has come back; cicadas sing,

Though twelve months silent, for

July is here;

And thou, O Aphrodite, void of fear,

Dost sport in gold; and thou, gold-hearted

thing,

O water-lily, drink'st (where reapers fling

Their serried loads of many a barbèd spear)

The scent of new-mown hay; and vague, yet

near.

The voices of the noonday chirpers ring.

The sky is blue and gold and pearl-besprent,

High blazes color, larkspur, poppy, pink;

The air is incense; it is joy to live;

Yet only soulless creatures are content.

Alas! in all this splendor we MUST think,

Beyond this beauty what has earth to give?

TO RICHARD WATSON GILDER.

OMES that sad voice, O poet, from
       your heart?—
That austere voice that vibrates on the strings
Of your sweet lyre, and into blithe song brings
Notes solemn, as if Christian chants should
       start
Into wierd concord with the notes that dart
From Pluto's bride in exile when she sings
Of woodland days, when near her mother's
       springs,
To Syrinx-music, she bade care depart:
In all your songs the birds and trees are heard,
But through your singing sounds an under-
       tone—

Wind-message through the reeds, not sung,

    but sighed:—

Your heart sings like a silver throated bird,

Your soul, remembering, sea-like, makes its

    moan,

Not for dead gods, but that the Christ has died.

OTHER POEMS

OTHER POEMS.

THE ANNUNCIATION.

HE shadow of palms is still, but stiller
the tall lilies' flame
(Emblems of Venus and Lilith), and
blazes the sun like a boss,—
A boss on the Archangel's shield hung in the
blue of the sky,—
For the Lady of Noon has arisen and
scattered her poppies abroad.
The flower narcissus is bending, drooping, yet
loath to die,
But the lilies are scarlet, defiant; they,
stately, with one accord,

157

Face the fierce gaze of the sun god, knowing
    no pain or shame,
  While fauns in the groves are moaning,
    mourning a nameless loss.

Where is there one spot of coolness, for all
    the wide earth seems dry,—
  Dry in the pitiless beating of sun-rays for
    many a day?
The sleeper beside the fountain that has no
    waters now,
  Sick of the scent of the poppies, sick of
    the sun's fierce glow,
Dreams of great torrents roaring, and, grate-
    ful, makes a vow;
  There breathes a sound celestial across
    the lilies' row,
From out the court of the Virgin; it turns
    the sleeper's sigh

Into a song of hoping, as the toiler goes
his way.

A serpent among the tall lilies raises his jew-
eled head
Spotted with scarlet color, ruby-like in
the sun.
" Air, or I die in this stillness!" the Tetrarch
cries in his tent;
"How silent the light is growing!" the
poet languidly sings;
And in the court of the Virgin a maiden's
form is bent,
Safe from the glare of the sunlight in the
splendor of seraphs' wings
That bear the Word of the Godhead; and the
Mystic Twain are wed,
As the voice of the Virgin murmurs:
" The will of our God be done!"

So soft,—and yet Nature wakens and the
    Hours from sleep arise;
So sweet,—yet the serpent quivers and
    dies in the scarlet sheen
Made by the flame-like lilies, no longer proud
    to the sun,
But sinking in shriveled death,—and a
    white cloud gently veils
The heat and the hate of Apollo, and the
    fountains once more run;
All Nature, the Mystic Mother with the
    gladness of new-birth hails;—
There stands the spotless lily where the crown
    of the red one lies,—
Love has struck the symbols of Lilith,
    and Venus is no more queen!

THE STRING OF THE ROSARY.

RBUTUS came from out the moist
    earth peeping,
And then a violet and a Bethlehem star;
And when a daisy smiled which had been
    sleeping
    Down in the pines, where sheltered cor-
    ners are,
The fields were hidden in a soft green cover
And our whole world was Lady April's lover.

The lilacs burst and filled the air with incense
    Then roses crowded in the way of June,
Beauties well guarded by their thorns and
    leaves dense,

Ruddy in daylight, pale 'neath harvest
    moon;
From pure white to deepest crimson ranging,
In loveliness from bud to blossom changing.

Then maples in the autumn! And the aster
    I saw last year its petals ruby red,
Gold-hearted, aromatic; fast and faster
      The year sped onward to the years that
        fled;
But gorgeous were the banners borne before
    him;
And clouds took purple vestments to adore
    him.

The last sad days were not so sad in passing,
    The barns were full, and hiding here and
      there,
A late flower bloomed; and to the eastward
    massing

Against the wind, the cedar hedges were

Green all the year, and greener in the winter;

Them ocean gales could neither bend nor

splinter.

These have their meaning; every month and

season

Speaks to the Christian heart a tale of love;

We, knowing this, in each may find a reason

For tender thoughts for the dear Lord

above;

Red roses say, " The Sacred Heart remember! "

" Eternal life! " cry hedges in December.

Poor is the man who sees but earthly flowers,

Hears only earthly voices in the trees,

And finds no symbols in the star-lit hours,

Though his great wealth be blazoned over

seas;

Poor! if he in the cloud sees only vapor

And in the sun a larger useful taper.

Fair silver lines the cloud of sternest duty,

    There is a glow on all our week-day deeds;

Through all the year there runs a string of

        beauty

    Like the bright chain that holds the

        rosary beads.

Life is not hard seen through the Resurrection;

Nature, read rightly, helps us to perfection.

THE ANXIOUS LOVER.

(J. K. E.)

SAW a damsel in a sombre room,

    Laid low in beds of purple violet,

And pale, sweet roses scenting all the gloom;

    And then I thought, This is a gray sunset

Of days of loving life. Shall he who stands

    Beside her bier, in sorrow for his love,

Be first in Heaven to clasp her gentle hands

To bow with her before the Lord above?

If love can die, let my heart be as cold

    As Galatea's was before the words

Of the warm sculptor drew it from the mould

    And made her hear the sound of singing

        birds;

Love's sunshine and love's shadows are they all
>Like April sun and shadow on the earth?
If love can die at sight of funeral-pall,
>Would I had strangled it in its sad birth!

I know that the sweet spring will surely go
>And leave no trace, except a blossom dry;
I know that life will pass as passes snow
>When March winds blow and river-floods
>>are high;
I know that all the maples on the hill
>That fire the air with flame to ashes burn;
I know that all the singing birds that fill
>The air with song to silent dust will turn.

Oh! love, my love, can it, then, ever be
>That thou or I may gaze upon love's death?
That thou shalt some day sad and silently
>Look on me dumb and cold and without
>>breath?

Or shall I see thee lying white and wan,

    Like yonder damsel in the flower-bed,

And only say, " My lady sweet has gone;

    She's lost to me; she's dead—*what meaneth*

      'dead' ? "

If love can die, then I will no more look

    Into thy eyes, and see thy pure thoughts

      there,

Nor will I read in any poet's book

    Of all the things that poets make so fair.

If love can die, the poet's art is vain,

    And thy blue eyes might well be blossoms

      blue,

And thy soft tears be only senseless rain,

    If love can die, like flowers and soulless

      dew.

I care not for thy smile, if love can die:

    If I must leave thee, let me leave thee now.

Shall I not know thee, if in Heaven high
    I enter and before the Holy bow?
Shalt thou not know me when before the throne
    Thou, white-robed one, shalt enter into
        light?
I cannot think the Lord of Love has sown
    His precious seed to make but one day
        bright.

Would I were dead, if death could be the end
    Of all the loving that makes life so fair!
If love can die, I pray the sun may send
    An arrow through my head, that death
        may tear
Away my soul, and make me soon forget
    The fair, sweet hope of love's eternal day,
Which yet might die like purple violet
    Strewn on the robe of her that passed
        away!

Ah! love, my love, when I look in thy eyes,

    And hear thy voice, like softened homely
        bells,

Coming to one who long has sent up sighs

    From foreign lands to be where his love

        dwells,

" The earth may crumble, but our love and we

    Shall live forever.   This is true! " I cry.

My heart lifts up itself in ecstasy.

    " Life were not life if our great love could

        die."

BETWEEN THE LIGHTS.

A PHANTASY.

(TO JOHN J. STAFFORD.)

IN the cool, soft, fragrant summer grass,
 In trembling stalks of white-tipped
  clover,
I lie and dream, as the shadows pass
 From twilight's gates the cloud-bridge
  over.

On the other side, dim other side,
 Lie starlight gloom, and the night's chill
  wind.
Calm Eve comes forth, like a timid bride,
 And with shaded eyes looks on mankind;—
She looks at me, as I lounge and dream;

She builds in the sky for my delight
High-towered castles that glow and gleam
    Redder than snow-crests in North fires
    bright.

She shows me Ceres in corn-flowers blue,
    And Pluto's bride on her throne below,
And Helen fair, to her lord untrue,
    Anguished and wailing in deathless woe;
Gold arabesques on a jasper ground,
    Gray cameo-faces, cold and grand,
Puck and Peas-blossom hovering round
    Oberon and his glittering band.

She changes her aspect, opal Eve!—
    Shows me a plain near the walls of Troy,
Where shepherds' sheep in low shrubs leave
    In haste, to gaze on a bright-haired boy—
The boy is Paris, he cometh out,

Out of the city, strong-limbed and fair.

Live I in future or past ? I doubt

Am I Greek shepherd or gay trouvère—

Who lieth, dreaming perhaps of her,

Œnone weeping for him, forlorn ?—

Who strives with the plaintive lute to stir

Some love in a Norman heart of scorn ?

Out of a balcon of hues that glow

There leans a lady against the sky;

Her robe is bordered with pearls, I know,—

Pearls on her neck with her pearl-skin vie.

There stands a lover in gay slashed hose,

With a bright plumed hat and purple cloak,

He calls her "lily" and "damask rose";

Even in cloudland they wear love's yoke.

Bold knights ride forward on prancing steeds,

King Arthur's court, with Sir Launcelot—

Presto! ' Tis Syrinx among the reeds,

    Apollo seeks her, but finds her not.

I am so idle in summer grass,

    I cannot think for scent of clover;

No moral I find in clouds that pass,

    I only know that sunset's over.

TO A POET IN EXILE.

(J. P. C.)

"I CANNOT sing!" the grieving heart-
harp sighed;
"The breeze that touched me lives beyond
the foam."
A rough wind struck it, and its voice replied
In sweeter music than it made at home.

O Sorrow, Sister Sorrow, thou dost give
A richer tone to poets when they cross,
To seek Eurydice, from where joys live,
And make them godlike through thy gift
of loss.

THE COUNTRY PRIEST'S WEEK.*

I.

(SUNDAY.)

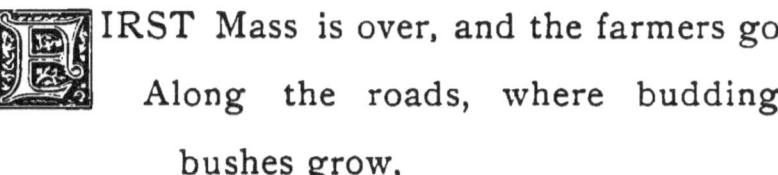IRST Mass is over, and the farmers go

Along the roads, where budding

bushes grow,

A sense of peace upon them,—"Winter wheat

Is fair to middling;"—as they meet and greet,

Their scraps of talk are not so full of gloom

As on the other days;—the wind-flowers bloom

In the sparse clearings, where the oaks are thin,

Among the puff-balls and the acorns;—in

A sheltered place arbutus shows its crest

Near where a meadow lark begins her nest.

*Suggested by Annette von Droste-Hûlshof's "Des Alten Pfarrer's Woche."

There is a stillness in the sunny air,
There is a quietness,—a softness rare—
The quality of Sunday—rest for all,
Except the priest, who answers to a call
From one in illness; last night till the moon
Late silvered the young wheat as light as noon
He heard confessions; betimes again to hear
The contrite tales he rose this morn; from near
And far the farmers gather;—fasting still
He greets them kindly, as he mounts the hill;—

He sees some neighbors as they churchward
            pass,
Who take his horse; and then he vests for Mass;
What time the farmers in their Sunday coats,
Talk of the weather, and count up the votes
For and against the party of their loves;
Their wives,—a little solemn in tight gloves,—
Exchange receipts and wonder if the beef

Will burn at home, and tell of joys or grief,

A recent death, or that a batch of bread

Came from the stove as light as thistle-head.

The Mass begins; the sad melodeon wails;

The Kyrie is sung; uncertain gales

Bear up the Gloria;—why will she who takes

The treble part raise high her painful "shakes,"

While alto, organ, and the bass profound,

Each independent, makes discordant sound?

Veni Creator!   Then the triumph comes!

The practice of a month that grand burst sums;

The basso roars, the treble, soaring, flies,

The alto trembles, sings alone, and dies.

On bended knees the old priest waits until

The warblers in the loft have worked their will;

"Veni Creator!" cry the four at once,

And then the basso (sure the man's a dunce!)

Repeats it and repeats it; then in turn

The treble and the alto show they burn

To rival his outpouring, till the priest

Is faint with weary waiting; and the feast

Of music falls in fragments in the air,

And somehow there is gladness everywhere.

A sermon on the duty of the time,—

The Easter time,—some Scriptural words sub-
lime

Of love and hope,—a wish about the pews

Whose rent is rather backward,—certain views

About a dance announced for Tuesday night,

In which plain speaking points the course of
right;

The young folks look ashamed, the elders nod;

" True to your Faith and you'll be true to God,

Which grace I wish you all."   A little while,

And all the place is radiant; angels smile.

Our Lord descends; the church is glorified;

The roughest face in some new flame is dyed;

The lights before the altar leap with joy,

The candles glow,—and that stout, red-cheeked
boy

Who holds the censer (to-morrow he will
plough)

Is rapt, seraphic, for a moment now;

The gray-haired priest is mightier than kings;

And this poor chapel, lacking many things,

Is grander than a palace: let them sing!

(Discords forgotten)—words of seraphs ring!

The Mass is done,—"Father, the banns next
week,—

Don't call them loud!" And then the widow
meek,

Approaching, stills the laugh; she comes to
seek

Another word of hope; her sad eyes speak

Of tears unshed,—"Father, a Mass?" she asks;

Then come some farmers, full of daily tasks,—

"Shall the new schoolhouse be of brick or

      stone?

Who will haul wood on Thursday? Is it known

Whether the railway passes Riley's field?—

But up the women glide—then the men yield.

A hasty dinner and a sorry one—

("The roast, you ought to know, is overdone.

And who can keep potatoes on the fire

Without their growing soggy? Thus the ire

Of her who guards the threshold of the priest

Takes form in words,—"You might have come,

      at least

Before the pudding burned; they chatter so!—

These country louts; they'd stop it if you'd go

And let them bite their tongues;—the gravy's

cold ")—

He eats and says no word;—the plaint is old.

And this grim lady (you have met her, sir?—

This guardian spirit?—here's success to her!)

Creeps to the door because a ring is heard;

"His Riv'rence is eatin',—can't you leave word?

No; you can't see him! Come to-night, I say.—

You can't?—well, try to come another day."

The door is slammed before the pastor can

Arise and stop the too persistent man

Who, when the supper waits "will come

again,"—

The guardian knows the wicked ways of men!

The Sunday-school—some words the priest

must say

To little children; and they must be gay,
Yet with instruction fraught,—a picture here,
A medal there, a smile for eyes that peer
From golden curls, a joke for that small boy,
A warning word for this: here, smiling coy,
The maidens come,—the altar needs repair,
And they will do it; then, with taste and care
He steers his way between the factions who
Hate all the good that other factions do.

Vespers and Benediction!—and the day
Of faith and love and all the various play
Of life in many tints, draws to its end.
The people in the sunset homeward wend,
And, in an hour, stern Martha lights the lamp—
("You've caught a cold, sir, standing in the
       damp")—
The pastor takes his chair. ("Old Clarke is
       here

About the money,—supper's spoiled,—that's
  clear!
And Mary Devlin wants,—Pat's at the door,—
I'll leave this house!—warning I give once
  more!")

The crowded day is gone; the lights are out,
The pastor rests at last; beyond a doubt
Pat Smith will come no more this night, at
  least!
And balmy sleep steals o'er the weary priest.
The day is done, well filled with duties, too,
And kindly thoughts and acts and sayings true.
He dreams a golden dream of heavenly rest; —
[Ah, broken dream! from out the lowering west
A man rides hastily, as the rain falls thick:
Three miles away, for Patrick Smith is sick!]

II.

(MONDAY.)

HE early Mass is said, the sunlight
glows

With tinge of red; the pastor homeward goes,

To pause a moment, just to say a word

To that old woman, whose sharp tongue,—he's
heard,—

Has made much havoc all the previous week,—

"You ask forgiveness, yet you evil speak,"

He says, with sternness; "at each morn you
rise,

In spite of wind and weather,—turn your eyes

In fervent ecstasy; you beat your breast,

And have not love;—of what avail's the rest?"

Abashed, the ancient dame, in shawl of black

And veilèd bonnet, sighs at this attack,

And hastens off, with bobbing courtesy short,

To face the parish with an altered port;

And he goes onward through the tender green,

Following a furrow in the changing sheen

Of winter wheat; the rain has passed away,

The new world glitters in a radiant day,

"Which God has given us!" he, reverent, says.

"How glad and glorious, O my God, thy
      ways!"

'Tis Monday, and his sermon's in the past,

And in the future,—freedom can but last

A day at most; no name is on the slate,—

There's an account, but those small bills can
      wait;

He scans the slate again; no letters mark

Its ebon surface;—there is Susan Clarke;—

He ought to see her, she's been ill, they say;

'Tis but a mile; he'll take it on his way

To "Jack Maginn's,"—forgive the "Jack" you
      can,

A priest's a priest, and yet a priest's a man.

For "Jack Maginn," now "Father," if you
      please,

Lives just four miles away, where willow trees

Bend o'er a garden, bound by mignonette,

And with a duck pond in an arbor set:

Here rose and cabbage in the summer time

Elbow each other; in another clime

Parochus learned to garden, by the sea

(There's shamrock under glass, kept carefully!)

In far-off Ireland,—(of his heart the pulse!)—

The only thing he can't grow here is *dulse*.

There was a time when "Jack" was young
      and gay,—

A player on the cornet, so they say;

He plays no more, at which his friends

rejoice,—

A seminarian with a tenor voice,

Who sang "The Minstrel Boy" and "Tara's

Harp";

But now his voice is just a trifle sharp

In the upper notes; one wouldn't care for

that,

If in the lower it were not so flat.

A man, like grave St. Paul, he holds no thing

Of boyish days,—except that he will sing.

The "Jack Maginn" of '60 is no more:

The cares of office, and the burdens sore

Of all the burdens of his little flock

Have changed him greatly,—yet there is a lock

That holds a secret portal, and the key

Is kept by him who journeys cheerily

Across the fields; behind this portal, bright
Are memories, and jokes, that saw the light
When Russell ruled at Maynooth,—of the
          young
And gifted cantors he had oft outsung!

The horse is stabled, and the old friends meet.
'Tis Monday,—you would know it as they
          greet;
"The ducks are in the stove, you'll stay and
          dine."
"Who talks of dining; it is not yet nine."
The arm-chair's out, the grate is made to glow,
And wreathes of fragrant smoke soft upward
          blow;
Now joke meets joke:—away, dull care, away!
For this is Monday, and a little play
Is good for men that think; the Office said
As far as possible; no work ahead.

Cigars and pews, the Bishop's health,—who
    spoke
At certain funerals,—(all of this in smoke,)—
The sermon of last Easter,—Hogan's boy,
("Gone to the bad,") and Jimmy Quinlan's joy
Over the rise in hay,—of course, the school;
And both agree that editor's a fool
Who in his leader took the other side
In Irish politics,—the man that lied
In last week's *Tribune* on old Froude's new
    book;—
And, for the season, how well all things look;

"Delaney and his tricks!" he died at sea,
Of yellow fever, caught in steerage,—he
Spent all the voyage among the sickened crowd
In the foul steerage; he was never cowed.
"Ordained a month!" And may he rest in
    peace!

A knock is heard; and now the talk must
    cease;

The ducks are ready, and a cook will wait

No more than time or tide, if men be late.

"The ducks are roasted." What!—already
    noon!

For once, at least, the diners dine too soon.

Nor is the day without its argument,

A wordy war,—the smoky air is rent

With *pros* and *cons* upon the Moral Law,—

"Père Gury says "—"In printing there's a
    flaw;"

"Yes!" "No!" "De Lugo!" "St. Alphonsus!"
    "Good,

Yet there's a gloss."— "No casuist ever
    could—"

"What nonsense!" "On the *Index!*" "In
    Le Pape

De Maistre says—" "Come, come, I'll take
    my nap,
If you mix history and 'Moral' so!"
And then our pastor thinks it's time to go.

But not till twilight where the wheàt is sowed
Turns green to gray does he take to the road,
Refreshed and strengthened for the coming
    week,
When life and death shall meet, and he shall
    speak
Most august words; now at his horse's head,
He quick remembers what he might have said.
"De Lugo settled *that!*" These words he hears
Hurled from the darkness, as the gate he nears;
He pauses, tempted; then into the gloom
Rides, laughing at the tempest in the room.

III.

(THE REST OF THE WEEK.)

HE swift week passes, each recurrent
        day
Brings a new duty,— lights and shadows play
Across the pastor's path; no rest he knows;
He feels the touch of joys, the weight of woes;—
On Tuesday, Burke the carpenter lies low,
The scaffold broke, a sudden fall, a blow;
From life to death the robust man is struck.
Happily for him there's neither fate nor luck;
He bows his head unto the chastening rod,
And, as a Christian, longs to meet his God.

Across the fields the anxious pastor speeds,
Bearing our God, to fill the poor soul's needs,—

And when the rites are over, and have ceased

The aspirations, and the soul's released,

The family turn in hope unto their friend;

"He's safe," the pastor says, "death does not

       end

Your life or his,—pray, pray, I pray you, *pray*,

And you shall meet him in the Light of Day!"

The candles fall upon the pallid face,

The family kneel; about them, peace and grace;

The soft tears flow,—ah, not in wild despair!—

There's golden hope; and why? *"The priest*

       was there."

He only of all men can do this thing,—

Tear from the mouth of death its poisoned

       sting!

Gentle he was,—but see him as he walks

Quick by the side of yonder man who talks

In maudlin nonsense,—angry is the word

He hurls upon the drunkard; who unheard
Excuse scarce murmurs, cowed, if not con-
      trite;—
Our pastor can be wrathful in the right!

On Wednesday there's a wedding,—nuptial
      Mass,
And then a warning word for lad and lass
The pastor speaks; a red-hued barn is cleared
For the great feast, a pine that late upreared
Its green boughs to gray skies is stripped and
      bare
To decorate a bower for the pair
Above the board, whose oaky firmness groans
Beneath the beef and fowl,—soon to be bones,
When hearty appetites shall circle round,
And cider sparkle, and tongues be unbound.

The farmers gather with their gifts and jokes,
And from the village come a crowd of folks,

Friends of the groom, (who keeps the village
store,

And stands uneasy, one foot on the floor,

Bashful, yet bold)—a strong hand lifts the
latch,

The priest has come,—'tis said he made the
match,

"And many others" add the chatting groups,

"All good ones, too." How coy the fair bride
droops!

Who'd think she'd helped with careful hands
to make

That center of her thoughts, the bridal cake?

The pastor reads these homely thoughts and
lives,

And into homely topics gaily dives.

"The bride looks well,—a little girl at school,—

Baptized her, sir.   But, come, the feast grows

> cool!"

And there's a rush, subdued a trifle, too,

When 'tis remembered that a "grace" is due;

He blesses the repast,—that farmer who

Sat down too soon, now rises, almost blue

With sudden flush; a laugh begins the chat;

A pleasant hour; the pastor takes his hat:

Full well he knows the meaning of the floor

Smoothed well and swept, and that behind

> the door

The fiddles wait; and young folks, too, the

> chance

Of cutting capers in a country dance;

How they protest! He must not go so soon,—

He'll wait till dark,—'tis easy—there's a moon

This time o' month,—the family all swear

They'll keep him by main force; but he must
tear
Himself away; he's not by this deceived,
He fancies that the young folks look relieved.

On Thursday there's the funeral,—sad and
slow
The neighbors drive their buggies, and talk
low
Of Wednesday's wedding, and the widow's way
Of getting on; the pastor bids them pray
For death in grace; "good deeds, not cease-
less plans
For money-getting, leave the pots and pans
And constant worry over kitchen stuff,
And pray each day; O friends, 'tis well enough
To live by bread, but not by bread alone,
Up, souls and hearts!" he cries, in pastoral
tone.

New resolutions move the serious crowd,

Our Lord descends, and every head is bowed;

God help the widow! — kind thoughts turn to

      her,

Born of his words, for well our priest can stir

The simple chords in honest hearts like these,

As well as quote St. Thomas. Through the trees

To the near graveyard goes the mourning

      train,

And prayers are fervent, though the soft

      spring rain

Falls on the clay that waits the sacred dead

And touches with its brilliants each low head.

On Friday childhood claims him, for he must

Go to the school,—such visits rub the dust

Of daily struggles from him,—now he smiles

And tells fine stories; many childish wiles

Are used to keep him there, the children know

That while he stays the hours will not go slow:

And when he's grave, the children love him
    still,

For, if he scolds, some pocket will he fill

With last year's walnuts, which will soothe
    the heart

That in the "First Commandment" got a smart.

And here comes Tom Malone,—his student
    boy,

To read a page of Virgil, and with joy

To hear the news that he may go in Fall

To some great college,—this will be a call

Upon the pastor's purse, but only one

Of many such. No wonder that the sun

Shows white on his best cassock, that the books

He loves are bought infrequent, that he looks

A little rusty in his Sunday dress,

When claims, like Tom's, on his resources press.

But God is good!—and Tom is grateful, too;

He'll stay all night and many a chore he'll do.

On Saturday, the sermon looms aloft,

A cloud upon the day,—alas! how oft

The pastor wishes it in retrospect.

At last 'tis done; (next week he will select

From out a certain drawer his Easter one,

Quite new, beloved brethren, for 'twas done

In eighty-two; 'twill fill the reverent fold

With holy awe; 'tis new because 'tis old!)

The church is chill; confessions must be heard.

The hour comes, it cannot be deferred;

He sits in patience, as the sun recedes,

Absolves the sinner, and the beggar feeds

With words that he alone, of all his kind,

Can use to cleanse the heart and soothe the

     mind,

And force repentant sinners to atone

With power that rests on no mere earthly
throne;
At night he waits, to hear the good-willed
men;—
His week has ended,—to begin again.

And thus from year to year his good deeds flow,
A crystal river, blessing as they go.
How many flowers spring up, like violets
In hidden clumps,—how many wild regrets
Are made content,—how many a sinful heart
Grows white again,—and so he does his part
In the great tragedy of human life.
A simple priest; and all his days are rife
With simple deeds; yet when the trump shall
ring,
None more rewarded in Christ's choir shall
sing.